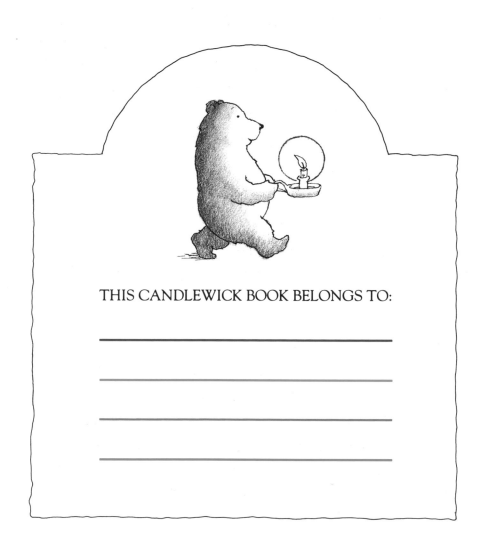

THIS CANDLEWICK BOOK BELONGS TO:

_____

_____

_____

_____

For Clyde Bulla—P. F.

For Greg and Jake,
True Weslandians—K. H.

First paperback edition 2002

The Library of Congress has cataloged the hardcover edition as follows:

Fleischman, Paul.
Weslandia / Paul Fleischman ; illustrated by Kevin Hawkes.—1st ed.
p.   cm.
Summary: Wesley's garden produces a crop of huge, strange
plants which provide him with clothing, shelter, food, and drink,
thus helping him create his own civilization and changing his life.
ISBN 0-7636-0006-7 (hardcover)
[1. Plants—Fiction. 2. Gardening—Fiction. 3. Civilization—Fiction.]
I. Hawkes, Kevin, Ill. II. Title.
PZ7.F5998We 1999
[E]—dc21   98-30240

ISBN 0-7636-1052-6 (paperback)

8 10 9

Printed in China

This book was typeset in Tempus Sans ITC.
The illustrations were done in acrylic.

Candlewick Press
2067 Massachusetts Avenue
Cambridge, Massachusetts 02140

visit us at www.candlewick.com

Weslandia

PAUL FLEISCHMAN

ILLUSTRATED BY
KEVIN HAWKES

CANDLEWICK PRESS
CAMBRIDGE, MASSACHUSETTS

"Of course he's miserable," moaned Wesley's mother. "He sticks out." "Like a nose," snapped his father.

Listening through the heating vent, Wesley knew they were right. He was an outcast from the civilization around him.

He alone in his town disliked pizza and soda, alarming his mother and the school nurse. He found professional football stupid. He'd refused to shave half his head, the hairstyle worn by all the other boys, despite his father's bribe of five dollars.

Passing his neighborhood's two styles of housing—garage on the left and garage on the right—Wesley alone dreamed of more exciting forms of shelter. He had no friends, but plenty of tormentors.

Fleeing them was the only sport he was good at.

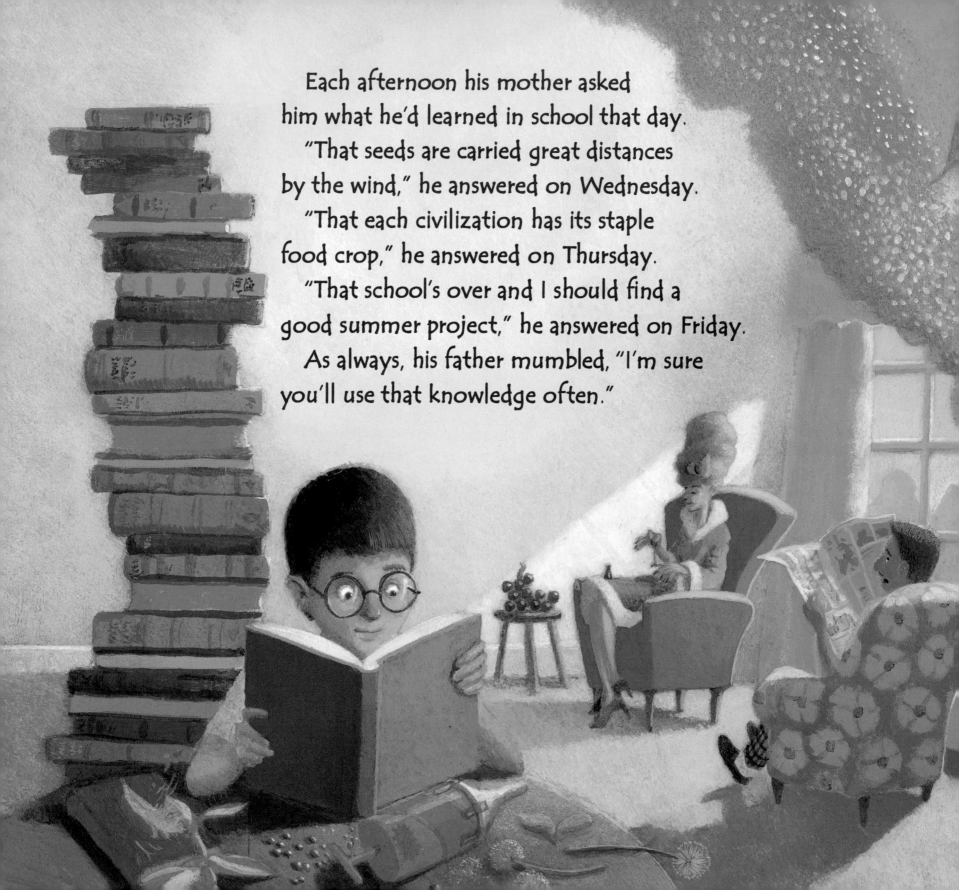

Each afternoon his mother asked
him what he'd learned in school that day.
"That seeds are carried great distances
by the wind," he answered on Wednesday.
"That each civilization has its staple
food crop," he answered on Thursday.
"That school's over and I should find a
good summer project," he answered on Friday.
As always, his father mumbled, "I'm sure
you'll use that knowledge often."

Suddenly, Wesley's thoughts shot sparks. His eyes blazed. His father was right! He could actually *use* what he'd learned that week for a summer project that would top all others. He would grow his own staple food crop—
and found his own civilization!

The next morning he turned over a plot of
ground in his yard. That night a wind blew in
from the west. It raced through the trees
and set his curtains snapping. Wesley
lay awake, listening. His land
was being planted.

Five days later the first seedlings appeared.

"You'll have almighty bedlam on your hands if
you don't get those weeds out," warned his neighbor.

"Actually, that's my crop," replied Wesley.
"In this type of garden there are no weeds."

Following ancient tradition, Wesley's fellow gardeners
grew tomatoes, beans, Brussels sprouts, and nothing
else. Wesley found it thrilling to open his land
to chance, to invite the new and unknown.

The plants shot up past his knees,
then his waist. They seemed to be all of
the same sort. Wesley couldn't find
them in any plant book.

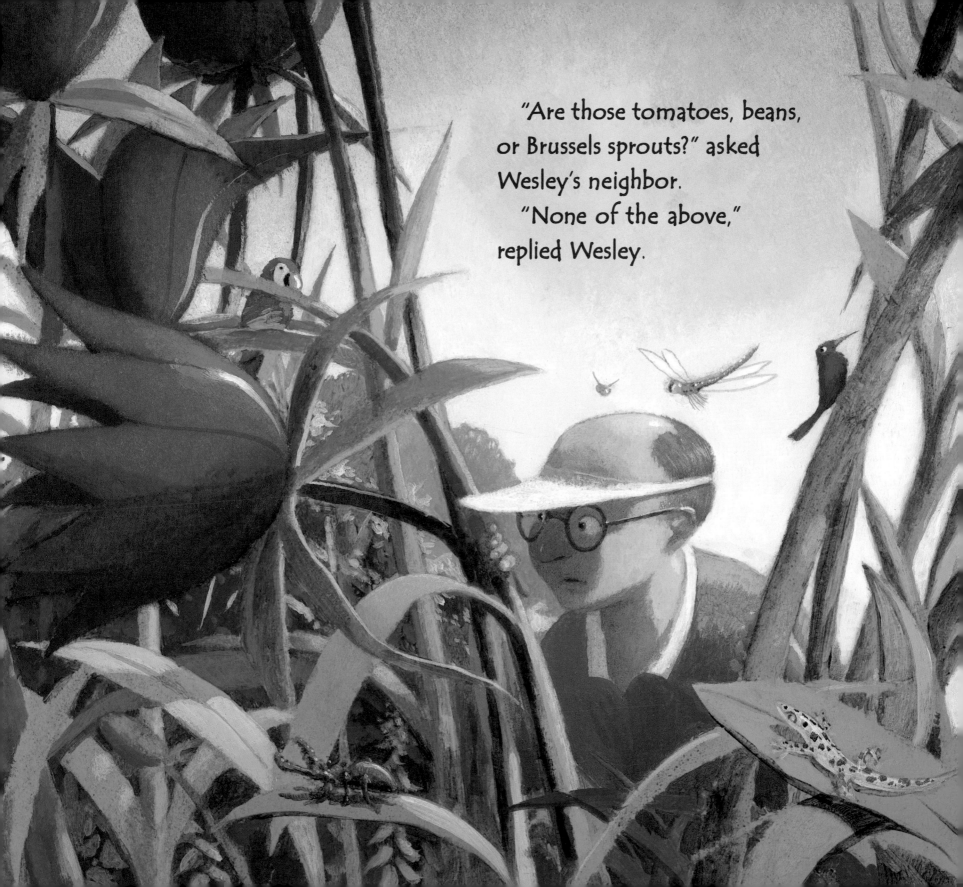

"Are those tomatoes, beans, or Brussels sprouts?" asked Wesley's neighbor.

"None of the above," replied Wesley.

Fruit appeared, yellow at first, then blushing to magenta. Wesley picked one and sliced through the rind to the juicy purple center. He took a bite and found the taste an entrancing blen of peach, strawberry, pumpkin pie, and flavors he had no name for.

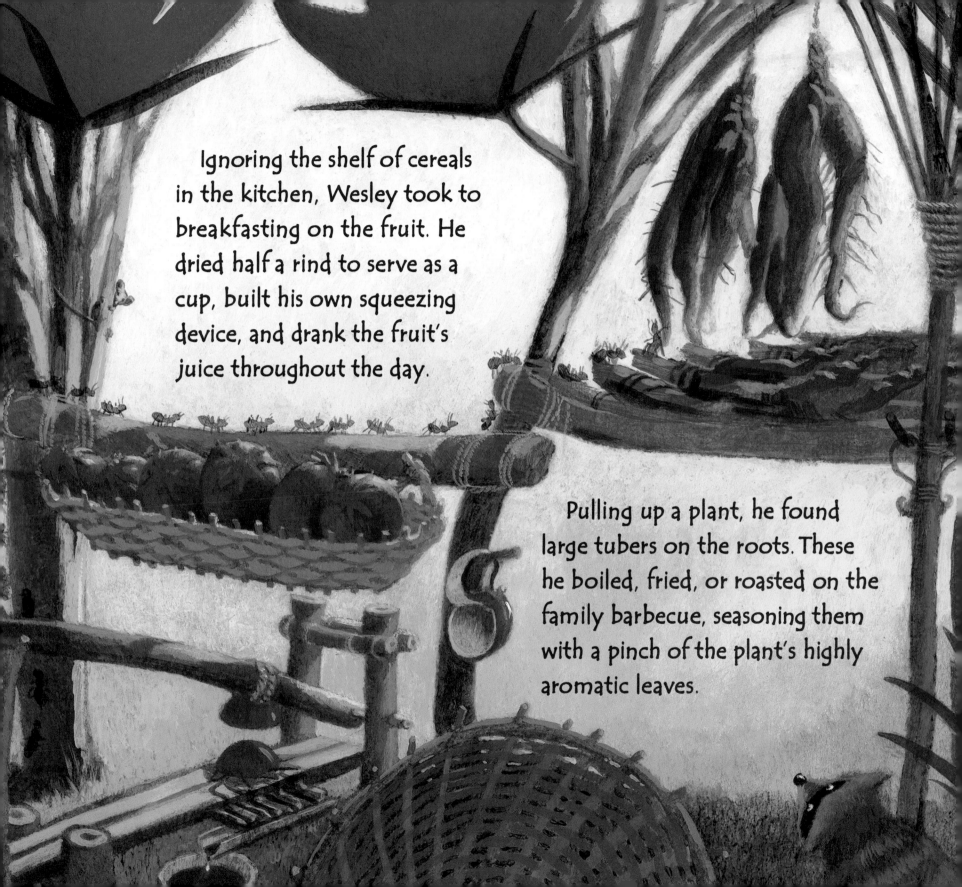

Ignoring the shelf of cereals in the kitchen, Wesley took to breakfasting on the fruit. He dried half a rind to serve as a cup, built his own squeezing device, and drank the fruit's juice throughout the day.

Pulling up a plant, he found large tubers on the roots. These he boiled, fried, or roasted on the family barbecue, seasoning them with a pinch of the plant's highly aromatic leaves.

It was hot work tending to his crop.
To keep off the sun, Wesley wove
himself a hat from strips of the plant's
woody bark. His success with the hat
inspired him to devise a spinning
wheel and loom on which he wove
a loose-fitting robe from the stalks'
soft inner fibers.

Unlike jeans, which he found scratchy and heavy, the robe was comfortable, reflected the sun, and offered myriad opportunities for pockets.

His schoolmates were scornful, then
curious. Grudgingly, Wesley allowed
them ten minutes apiece at his mortar,
crushing the plant's seeds to collect the oil.
This oil had a tangy scent and served
him both as suntan lotion and mosquito
repellent. He rubbed it on his face each
morning and sold small amounts to his
former tormentors at the price of ten
dollars per bottle.

"What's happened to your watch?" asked his mother one day.

Wesley admitted that he no longer wore it. He told time by the stalk that he used as a sundial and had divided the day into eight segments— the number of petals on the plant's flowers.

He'd adopted a new counting system as well, based likewise upon the number eight. His domain, home to many such innovations, he named

"Weslandia."

Uninterested in traditional sports, Wesley made up his own. These were designed for a single player and used many different parts of the plant. His spectators looked on with envy.

Realizing that more players would offer him more scope, Wesley invented other games that would include his schoolmates, games rich with strategy and complex scoring systems. He tried to be patient with the other players' blunders.

August was unusually hot. Wesley
built himself a platform and took to
sleeping in the middle of Weslandia.
He passed the evenings playing a flute
he'd fashioned from a stalk or gazing up
at the sky, renaming the constellations.

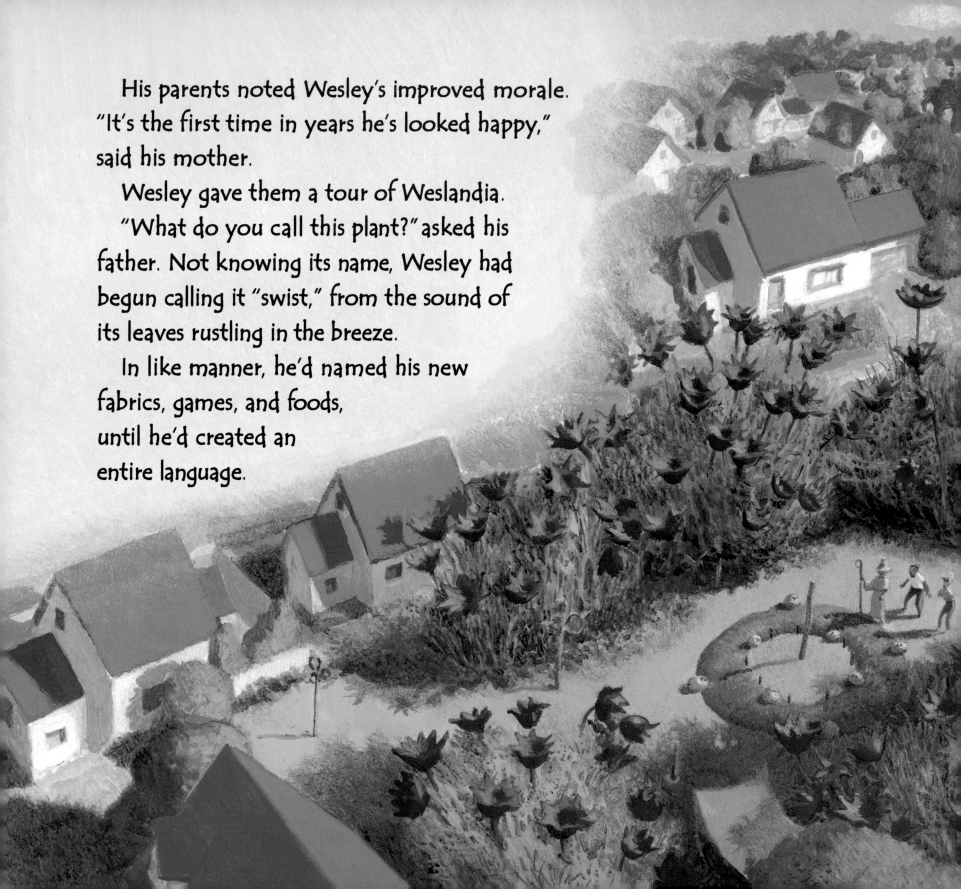

His parents noted Wesley's improved morale. "It's the first time in years he's looked happy," said his mother.

Wesley gave them a tour of Weslandia.

"What do you call this plant?" asked his father. Not knowing its name, Wesley had begun calling it "swist," from the sound of its leaves rustling in the breeze.

In like manner, he'd named his new fabrics, games, and foods, until he'd created an entire language.

Mixing the plant's oil with soot,
Wesley made a passable ink. As the finale
to his summer project, he used the ink and
his own eighty-letter alphabet to record
the history of his civilization's founding.

In September, Wesley returned to school . . .

He had no shortage of friends.

PAUL FLEISCHMAN, like Wesley, constructed his own alternate world during his school years. "My friends and I invented our own sports, ran an underground newspaper, and created our own school culture," he says. "It was fine training. Writing books—each an alternate universe—is now my daily endeavor." Paul Fleischman is the award-winning author of many books for children and young adults, including *Big Talk: Poems for Four Voices*; *Joyful Noise: Poems for Two Voices*, winner of the Newbery Medal; *Graven Images*, a Newbery Honor Book and an American Library Association Notable Children's Book; *Bull Run*, winner of the Scott O'Dell Award for historical fiction; *Saturnalia*, a *Boston Globe–Horn Book* Honor Book and an American Library Association Notable Book; and *Dateline: Troy*, an American Library Association Best Book for Young Adults. He lives in California.

KEVIN HAWKES found Wesley's world particularly intriguing and says that it reminded him of *Robinson Crusoe*, one of his favorite books as a child. "Wesley lives in this suburban place where everything is the same," he explains, "yet he has created something unique and is living self-sufficiently on his own island, in a way." Kevin Hawkes is the illustrator and author-illustrator of a number of popular books for children, including *Handel, Who Knew What He Liked*; *My Little Sister Ate One Hare*; *The Librarian Who Measured the Earth*; *Marven of the Great North Woods*; and *Painting the Wind: A Story of Vincent Van Gogh*. He lives with his family in Maine.